MASCOT BOOKS

www.mascotbooks.com

©2013 Wells Brothers, LLC. All Rights Reserved. No part of this publication may be reproduced, stored in a retrieval system or transmitted in any form by any means electronic, mechanical, or photocopying, recording or otherwise without the permission of the author.

For more information, please contact:
Mascot Books
560 Herndon Parkway #120
Herndon, VA 20170
info@mascotbooks.com

CPSIA Code: PRT0913A
ISBN-10: 1620862956
ISBN-13: 9781620862957

All the university indicia are protected trademarks or registered trademarks of their respective institutions and are used under license.

Printed in the United States

THAT'S NOT OUR MASCOT?
Rebel is Our Mascot

Ole Miss

by Jason Wells and Jeff Wells

illustrated by Patrick Carlson

Who's that tailgating in the Grove?

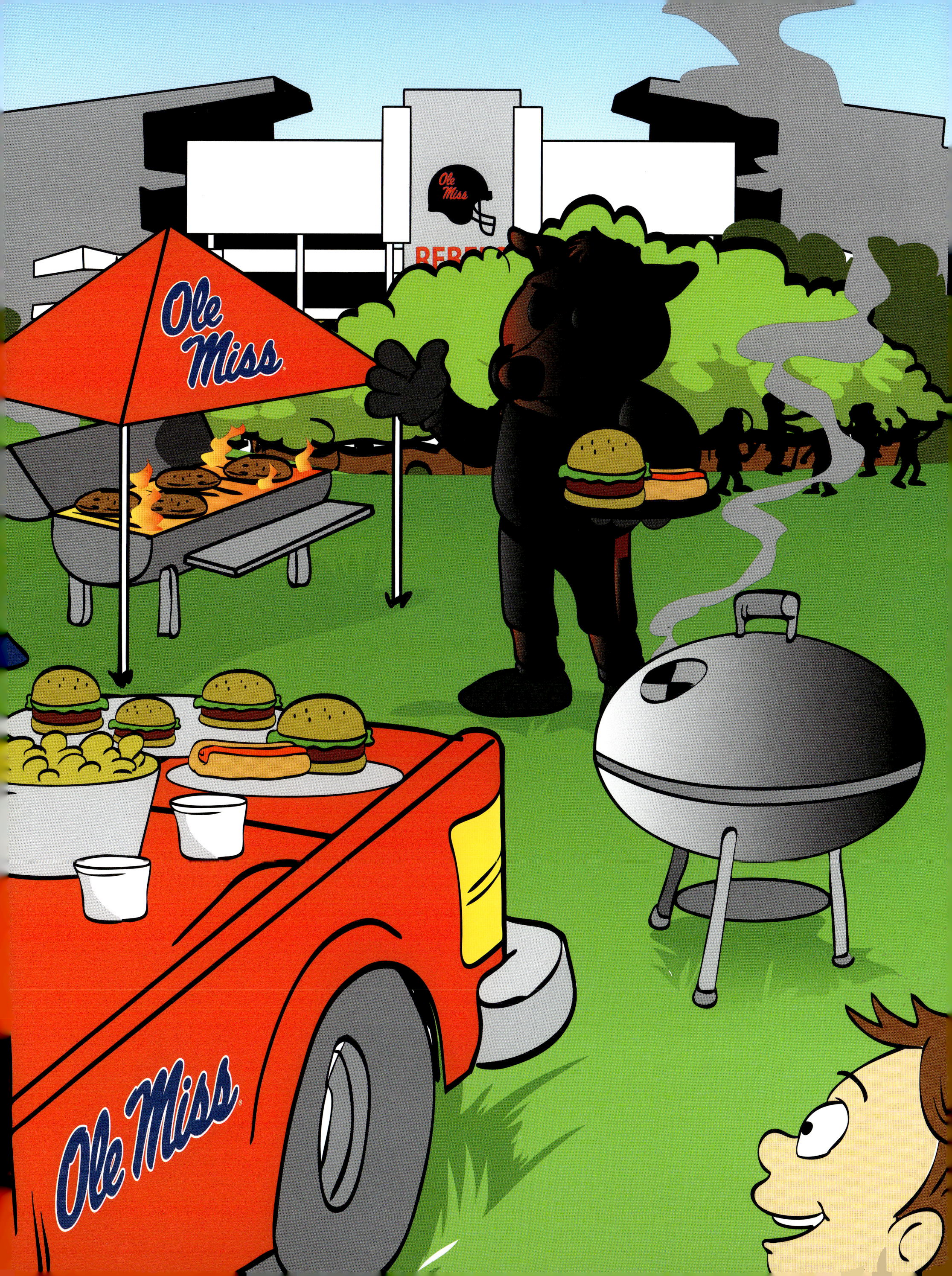
Ole Miss
Ole Miss
Ole Miss

That's not our mascot...
it's Big Red, the Arkansas Razorback.

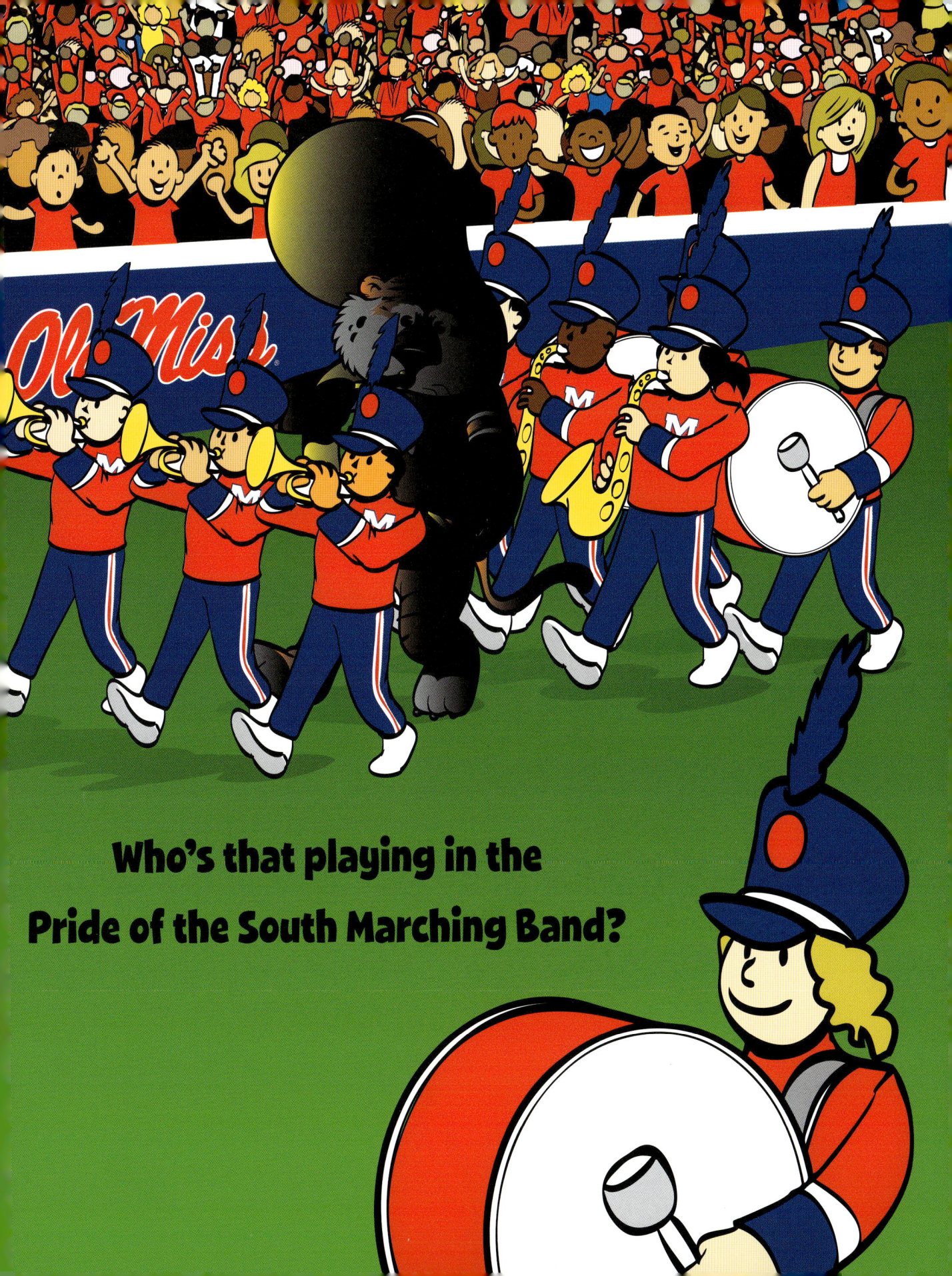

Who's that playing in the Pride of the South Marching Band?

That's not our mascot...
it's Aubie, the Auburn Tiger.

Ole Miss

Who's that shooting hoops in Tad Smith Coliseum?

That's not our mascot...
it's Albert, the Florida Gator.

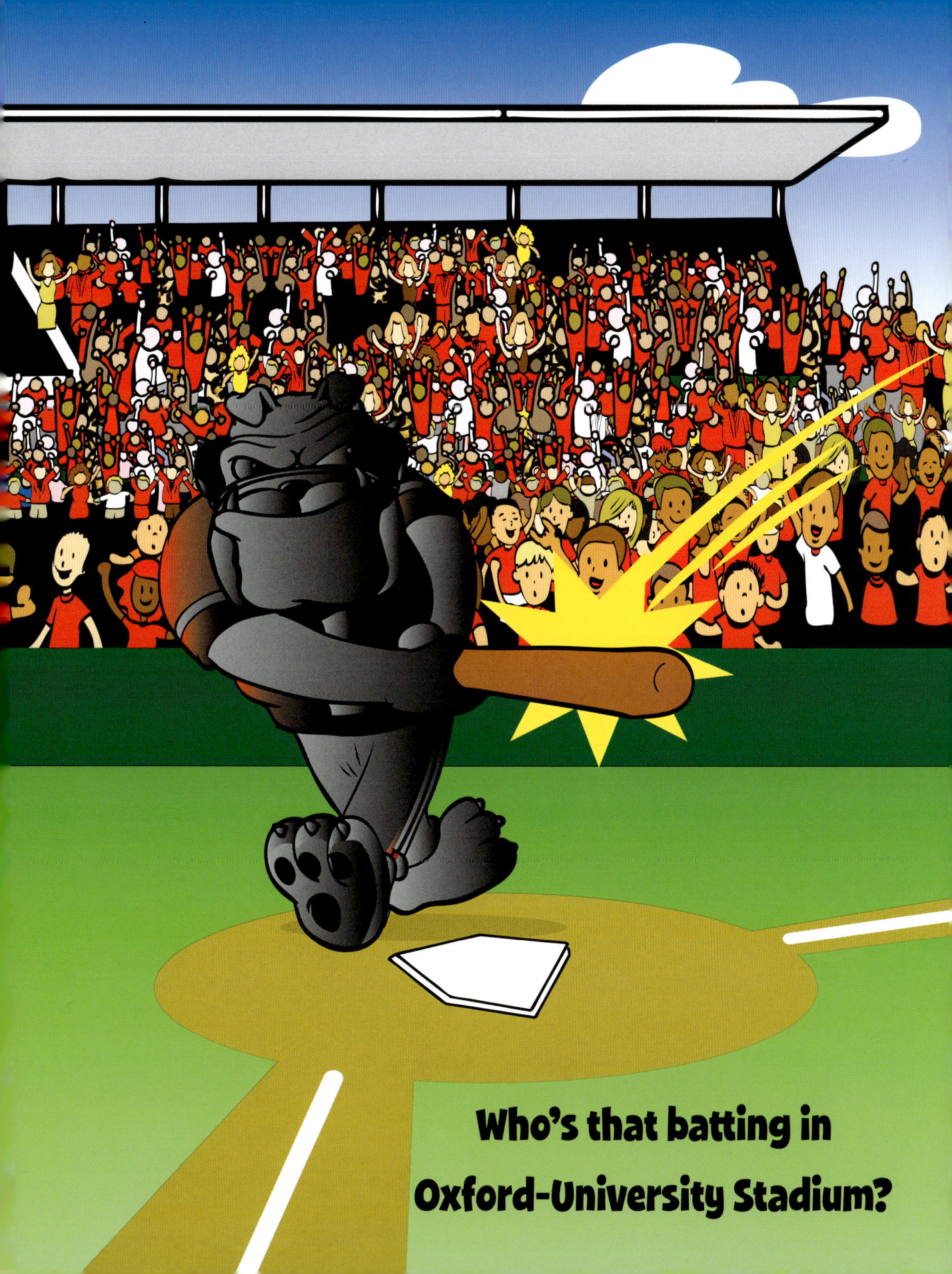

Who's that batting in Oxford-University Stadium?

That's not our mascot...
it's Hairy Dawg,
the Georgia Bulldog.

Who's that leading the Walk of Champions?

WALK OF CHAMPIONS

That's not our mascot...
it's Scratch, the Kentucky Wildcat.

Who's that performing at the Ford Center?

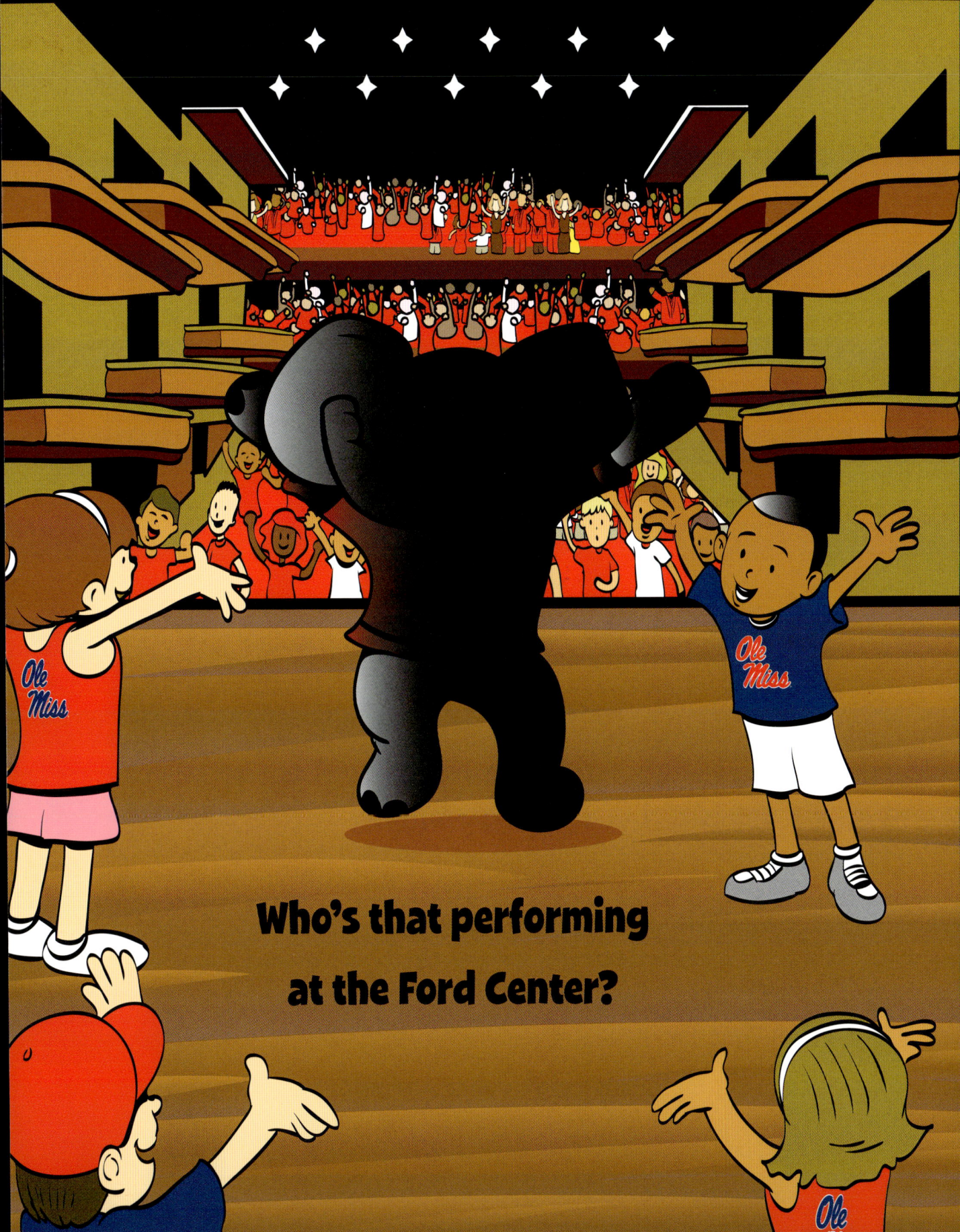

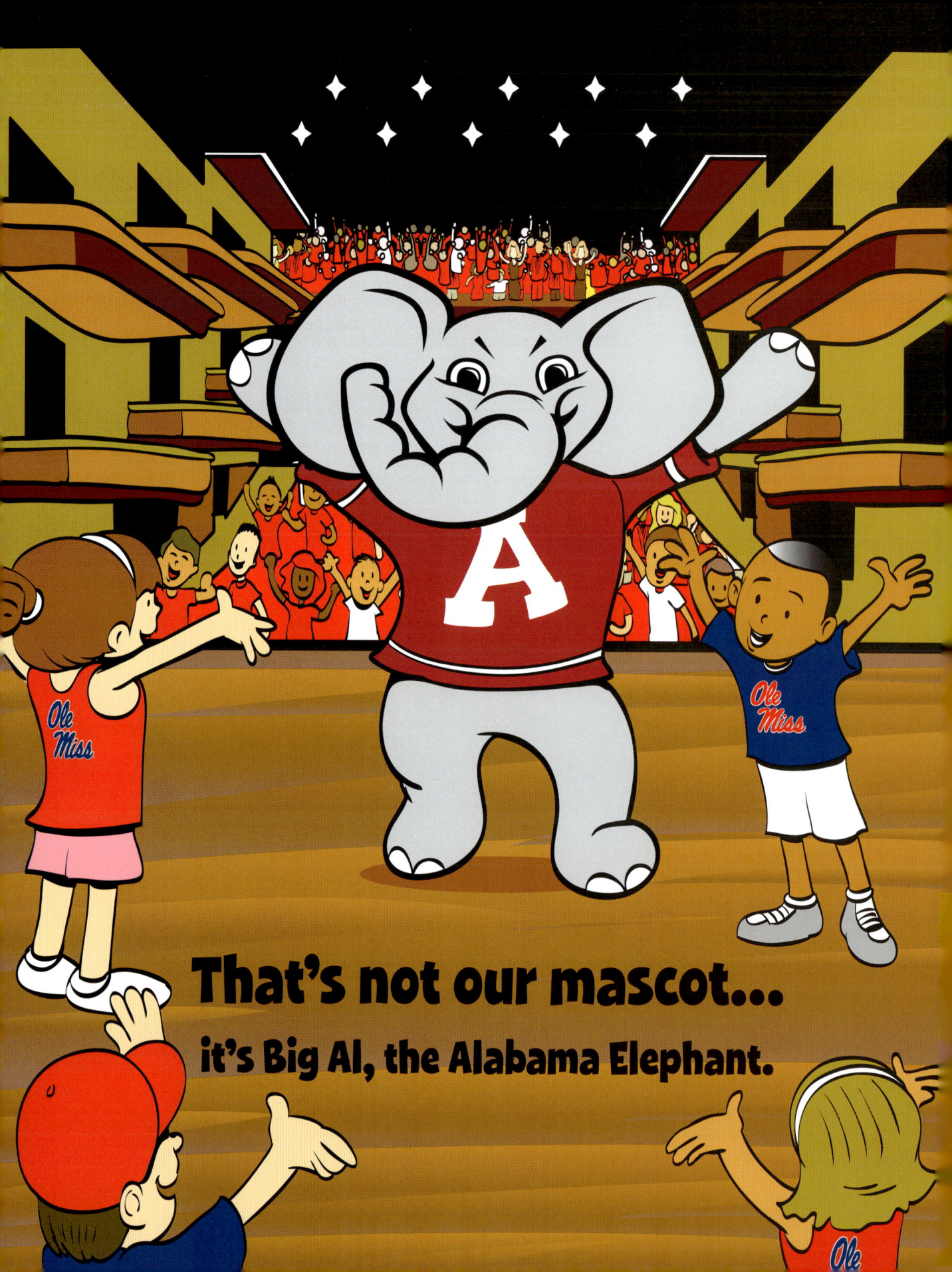

That's not our mascot...

it's Big Al, the Alabama Elephant.

Who's that eating at the Union?

That's not our mascot...
it's Mike, the LSU Tiger.

Who's that working out at the Turner Center?

That's not our mascot...
it's Bully, the Mississippi State Bulldog.

Who's that playing by the Central Fountain?

That's not our mascot...
it's Truman, the Missouri Tiger.

Who's that reading
The Daily Mississippian?
The Daily Mississippian
Ole Miss

That's not our mascot...

it's Cocky, the South Carolina Gamecock.

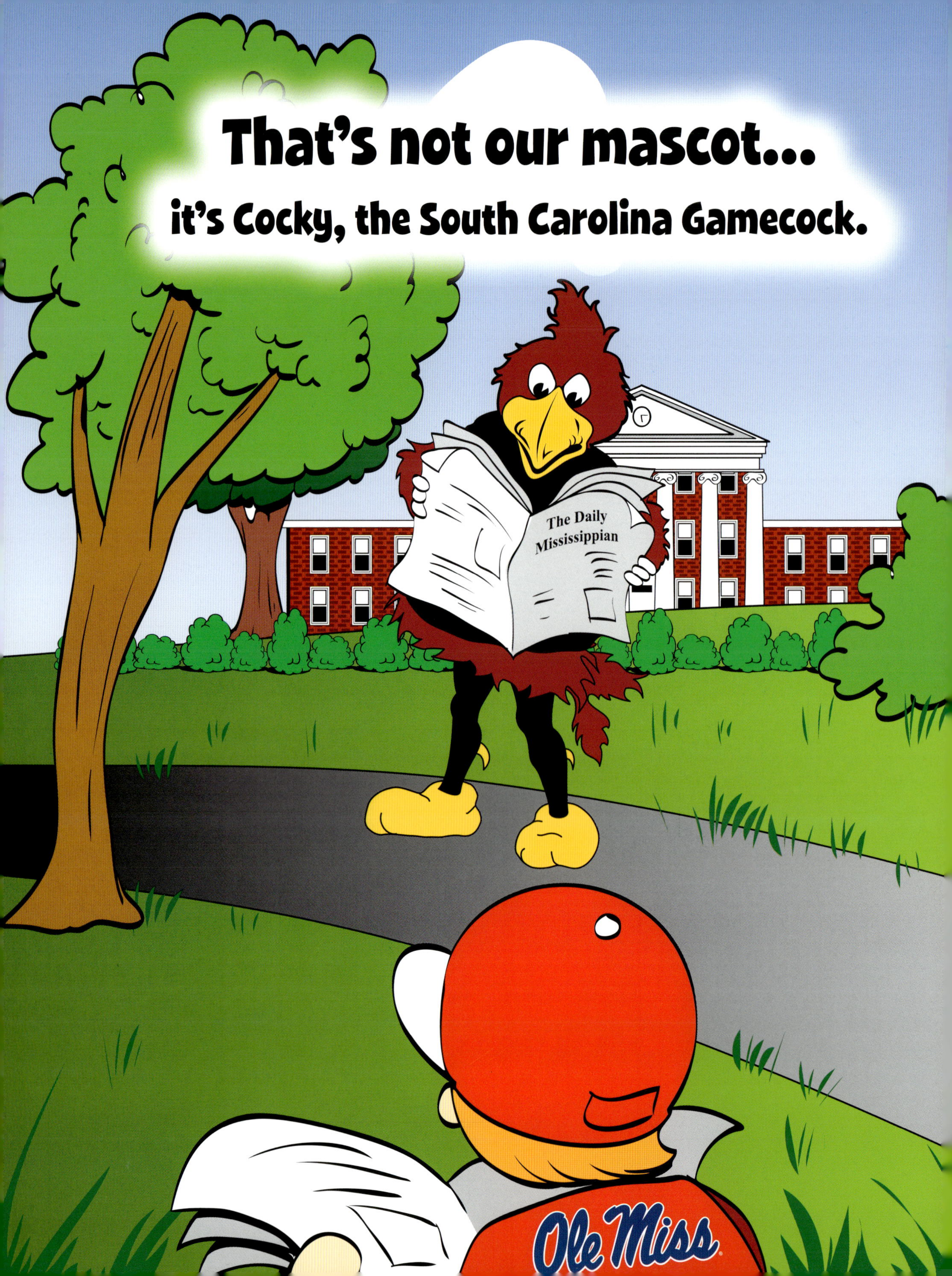

Who's that studying at the Williams Library?

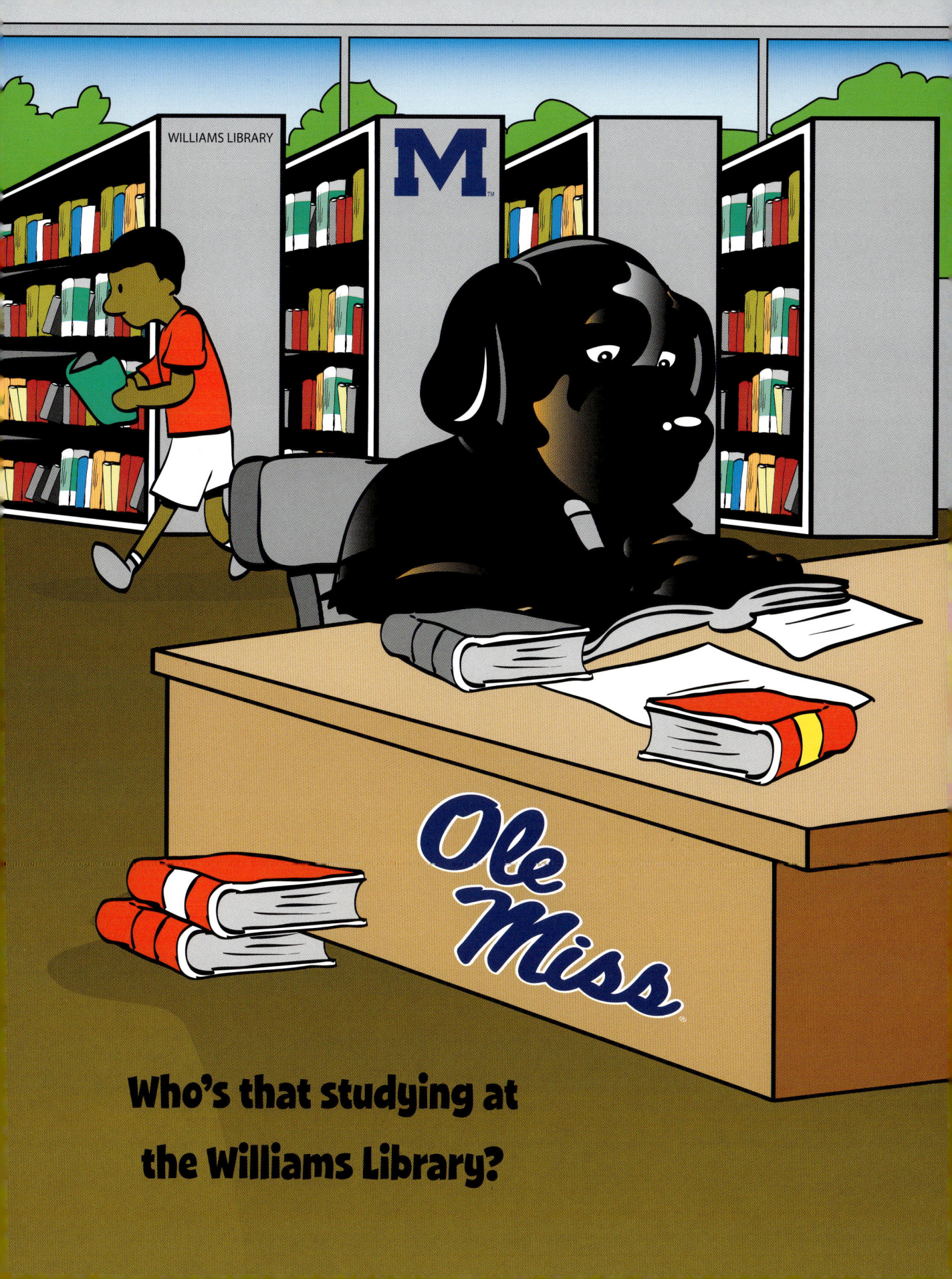

That's not our mascot...
it's Smokey, the Tennessee Volunteer.

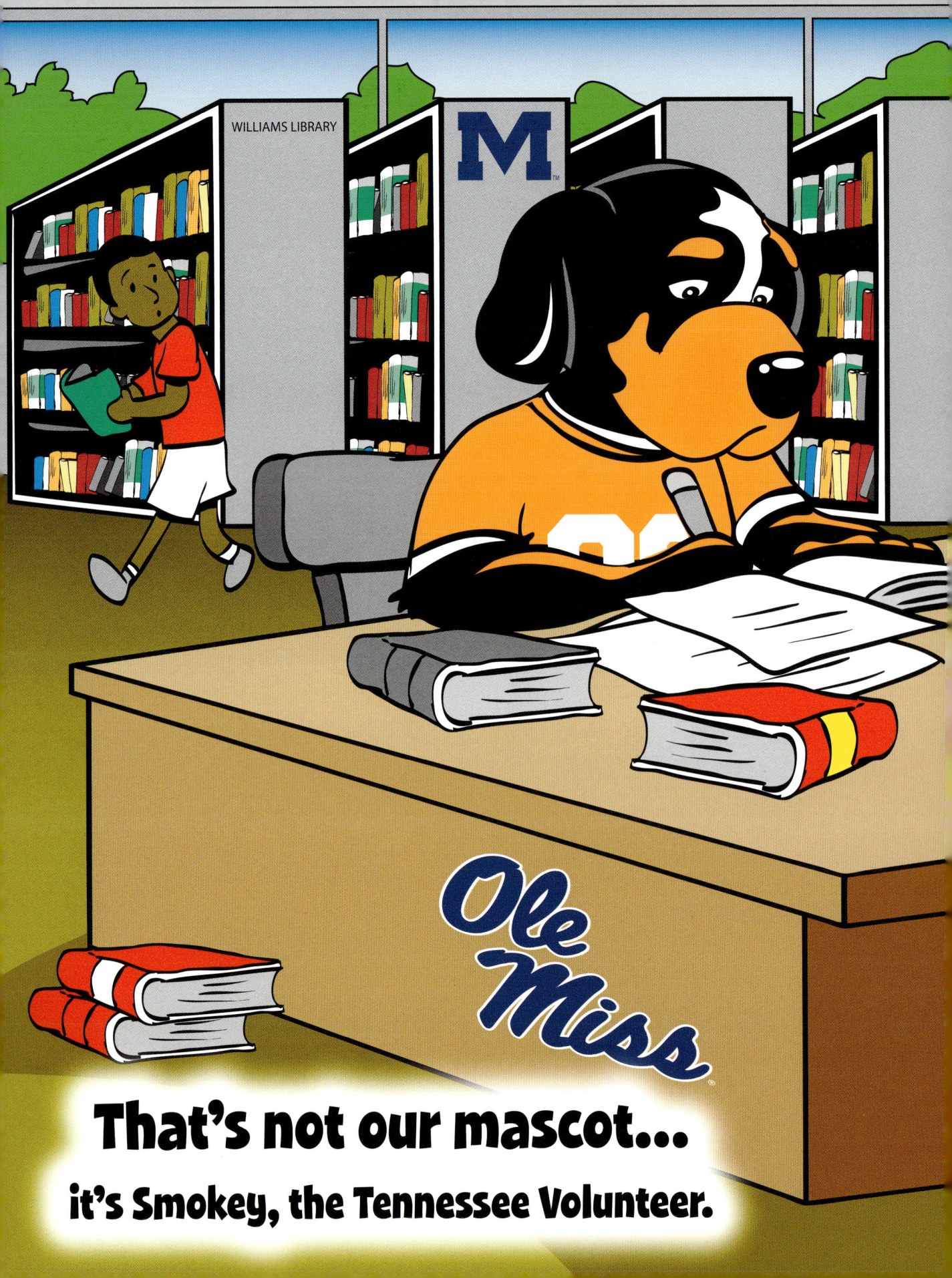

Who's that visiting Rowan Oak?

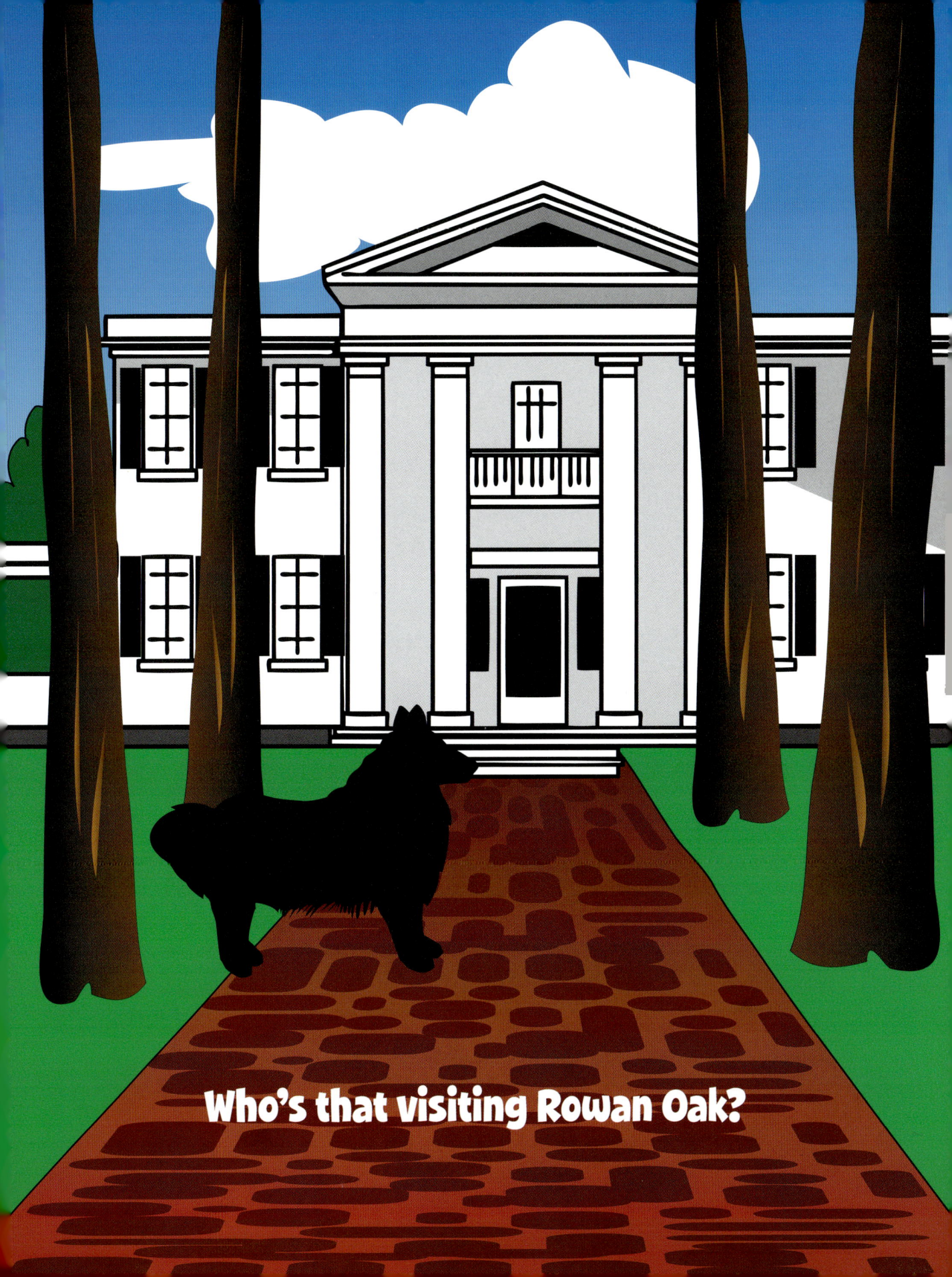

That's not our mascot...

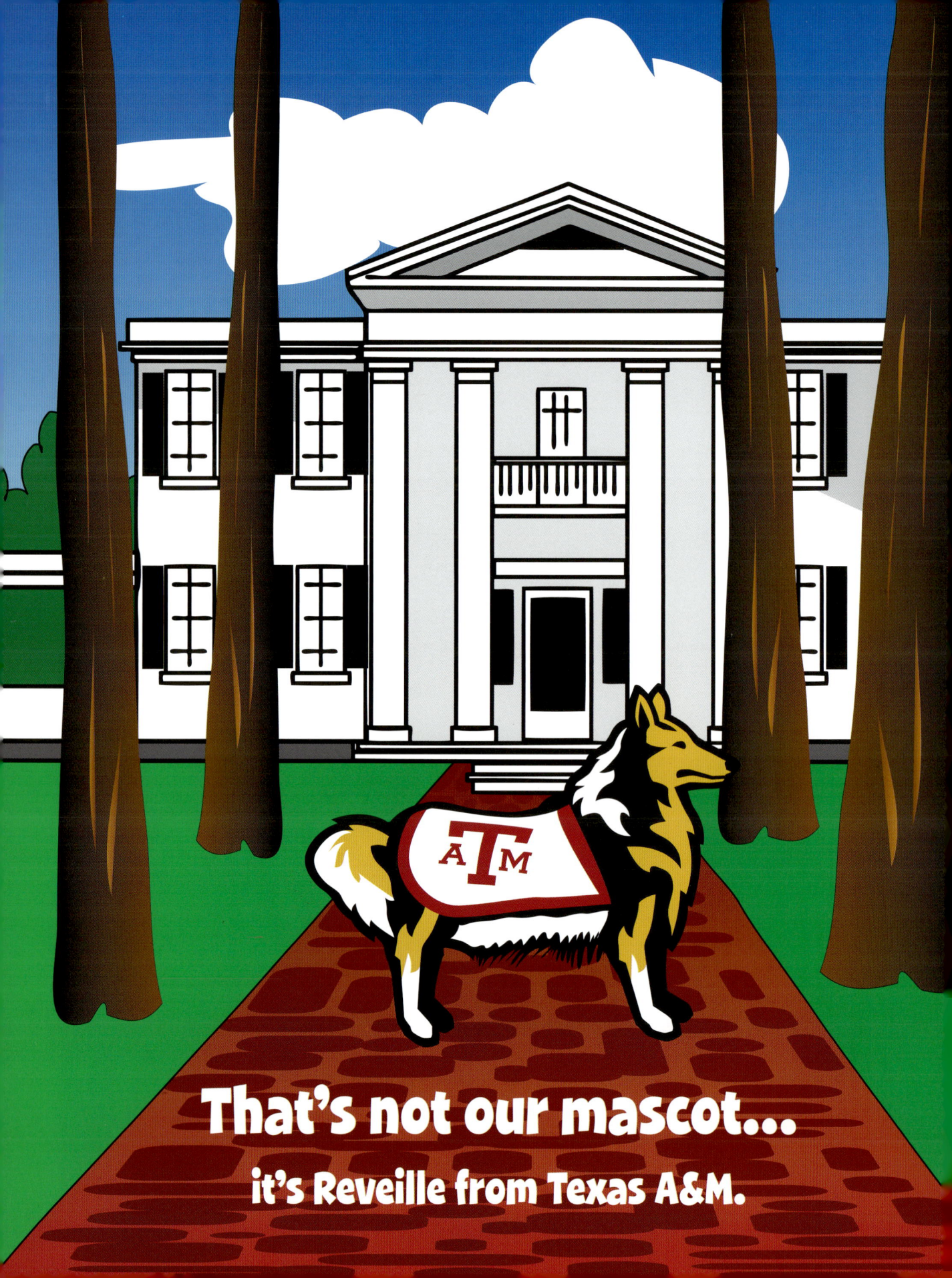

it's Reveille from Texas A&M.

Who's that strolling by the Lyceum?

That's not our mascot...
it's Mr. C, the Vanderbilt® Commodore.

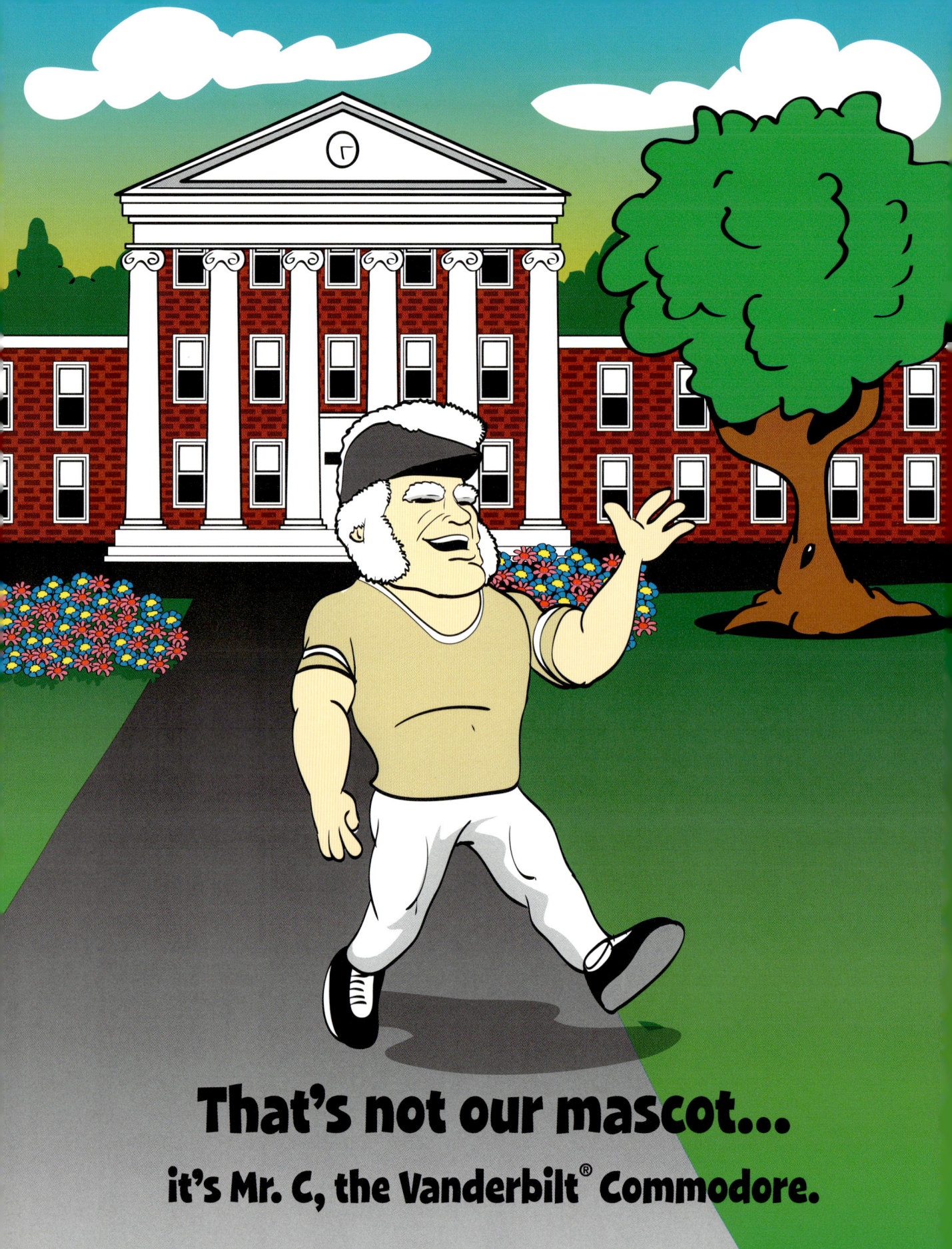

"Hotty Toddy"

Who's that yelling "Hotty Toddy" in Vaught-Hemingway Stadium?

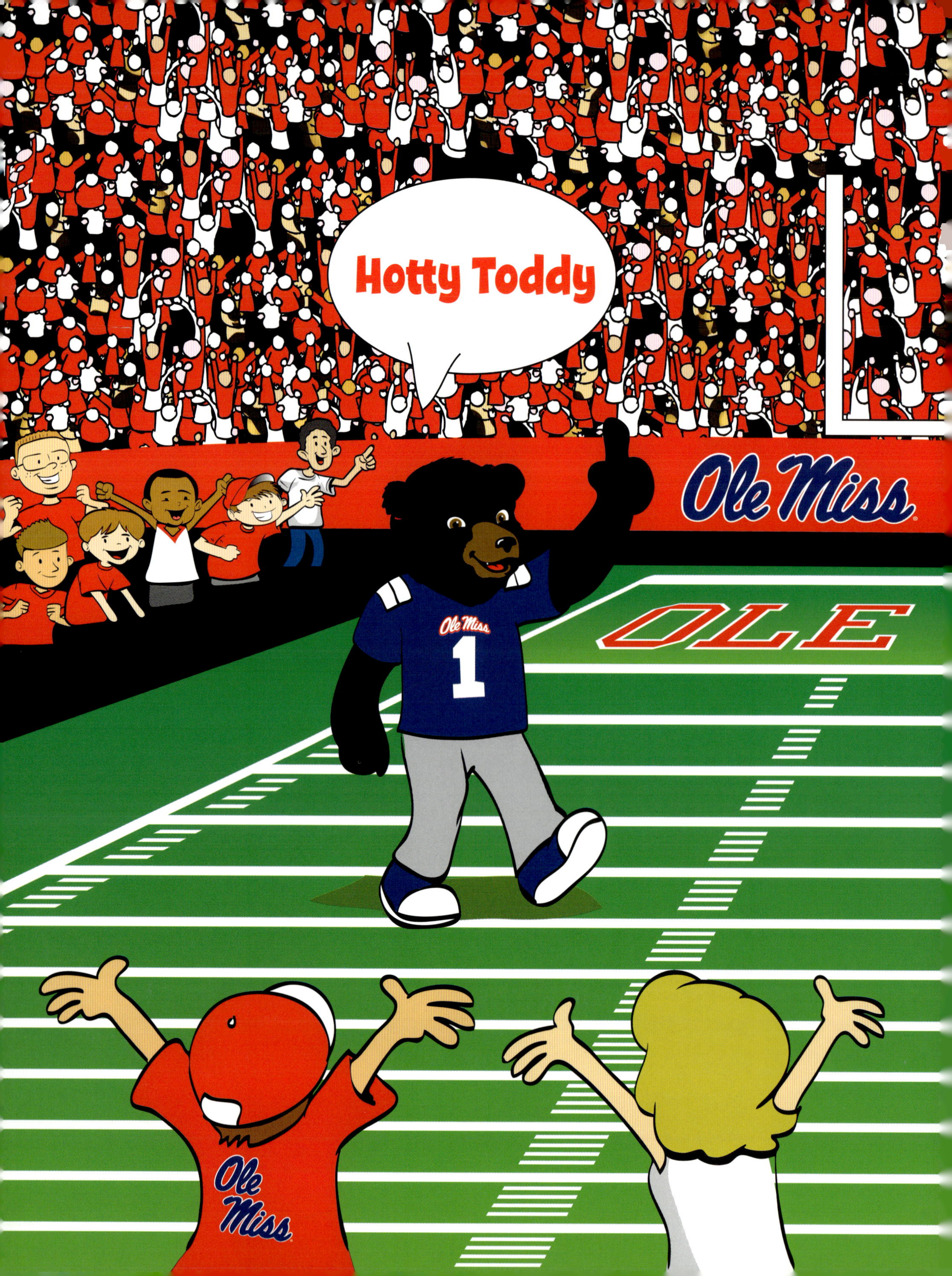
Hotty Toddy
Ole Miss
OLE
Ole Miss
1
Ole Miss

THAT'S OUR MASCOT... it's Rebel, the Ole Miss Black Bear!